Topic: Animals   **Subtopic:** Pet Animals

Notes to Parents and Teachers:

It is an exciting time when a child begins to learn to read! Creating a positive, safe environment to practice reading is important to encourage children to love to read.

REMEMBER: PRAISE IS A GREAT MOTIVATOR!

Here are some praise points for beginning readers:

- You matched your finger to each word that you read!
- I like the way you used the picture to help you figure out that word.
- I love spending time with you listening to you read.

Book Ends for the Reader!

Here are some reminders before reading the text:

- Carefully point to each word to match the words you read to the printed words.

- Take a 'picture walk' through the book before reading it to notice details in the illustrations. Use the picture clues to help you figure out words in the story.

- Get your mouth ready to say the beginning sound of a word to help you figure out words in the story.

Words to Know Before You Read

dog

elephant

giraffe

hamster

messy

scary

snake

tiger

The Perfect PET

By Carl Nino

Illustrated by
Isabella Grott

Rourke
Educational Media
rourkeeducationalmedia.com

I want a pet.

What will I get?

How about a giraffe?

No, no, no! It is too tall.

How about an elephant?

No, no, no! It is too big.

How about a tiger?

No, no, no! It is too scary.

How about a snake?

No, no, no! It is too long.

How about a dog?

No, no, no! It is too messy.

How about a hamster?

Yes, yes, yes! It is cute.

It is not too big or too scary.

It is not too long or too messy.

I like a hamster.

It is the perfect pet.

Book Ends for the Reader

I know...

1. Which animal is too tall?

2. Which animal is too big?

3. Which animal is too scary?

I think ...

1. Do you like animals?

2. What is your favorite animal?

3. Do you have a pet? If so, what kind?

Book Ends for the Reader

What happened in this book?

Look at each picture and talk about what happened in the story.

About the Author

Carl Nino is an avid reader and loves writing about all kinds of things. He loves to travel and is trying to visit as many countries as he can. He enjoys learning about the different cultures and traditions of people all around the world!

About the Illustrator

Isabella was born in 1985 in Rovereto, a small town in northern Italy. As a child she loved to draw, as well as play outside with Perla, her beautiful German Shepherd. She studied at Nemo Academy of Digital Arts in the city of Florence, where she currently lives with her cat, Miss Marple. Isabella also has other strong passions: traveling, watching movies and reading—a lot!

Library of Congress PCN Data

The Perfect Pet / Carl Nino

ISBN 978-1-68342-703-2 (hard cover)(alk.paper)
ISBN 978-1-68342-755-1 (soft cover)
ISBN 978-1-68342-807-7 (e-Book)
Library of Congress Control Number: 2017935349

Rourke Educational Media
Printed in the United States of America, North Mankato, Minnesota

Edited by: Debra Ankiel
Art direction and layout by: Rhea Magaro-Wallace
Cover and interior Illustrations by: Isabella Grott